Make it...
GROW

Written by Gordon Volke

TOP THAT! Kids

Getting Started

You don't need a garden for gardening! You can have lots of fun making things grow indoors!

The good things about gardening are that it's exciting and interesting, it's very cheap, and most of the time you can do it on your own.

There's nothing nicer than seeing the things you've planted sprouting into growth. It's also amazing to watch the way in which they grow.

Everything you need to start your indoor garden is contained in your special fun kit. Follow any of the ideas in this book and you'll find you can grow something really cool.

Gardening can keep you occupied for hours. Provided an adult knows what you're doing, you can have a wonderful time by yourself or working with friends.

This book is packed with fun ideas for you to try. Go on... go for it. GROW FOR IT!

What's in the Kit?

Propagator

This plastic box with a clear lid is used for growing plants. All you have to do is fill it with compost into which you plant seeds.

Dibble

"Dib" means to "dip" or to "dig." Your dibble is a tool that is used to make small holes in the compost into which you put the seeds.

Pots and saucers

When your plants grow bigger, they need to be moved to the flowerpots so they can grow strong roots. Stand the pots in the saucers and fill them with water to give your young plants a drink.

Tags and stickers

All tiny plants look very alike. To help you remember what you have planted, write the plant's name or draw a picture on the stickers. Press the stickers onto the tags and put them near your seeds to remind you what they are.

You will also need:

- compost—this is cheap to buy and can be found in any hardware store or nursery.
- seeds—don't go for the most exciting picture on the packet as these plants will probably be difficult to grow!
- a watering can

Gardening Guidelines

Gardening is cool, but to avoid upsetting your mom or dad, just follow these simple rules.

PLEASE DO

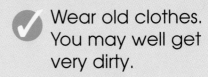

✓ Wear old clothes. You may well get very dirty.

✓ Ask permission before you borrow any tools —and put them back!

✓ Clean up after you have finished working and wash your hands.

✓ Be prepared to wait. Plants and flowers don't grow instantly. It may take weeks or even months before you see results!

X Go in the garage or basement where there may be dangerous chemicals, without an adult.

X Forget your plants after you have made them up into displays. Most will need watering from time to time.

X Treat your plants and flowers like objects. They are living things. Get to know their different needs, learn how to look after them and, above all, give them lots of love!

X Use anything pointed or sharp. Some ideas in this book require you to do some digging or cutting. They have been marked with this warning: NEEDS ADULT HELP! Look out for it!

Plants and Flowers

Before you start growing them, there are some interesting things you can learn about plants and flowers.

Did you know that...

1 There are more than 350,000 different kinds of plants in the world.

2 Trees are plants—the biggest plants reach right up to the sky.

3 The smallest plant can only be seen through a microscope.

4 Plants are great survivors. They can grow on cold, windswept mountains or in burning hot deserts.

5 Plants also grow in the sea.

Wild flowers in the desert

An underwater plant—a purple tube sponge.

Why are plants important?

Plants are a vitally important part
of life on Earth because...

1 They give out oxygen which is
breathed by animals and humans.

2 They provide food for animals and
humans.

3 Lots of everyday things are made
from plants, including paper,
cotton, and some furniture.

A sweet chestnut tree.

How do plants grow?

1 The ROOTS keep the plant firmly fixed in the soil. They also allow the plant to take in water and other chemicals to make it grow strong.

Bright red flowers of the gerbera plant.

2 The STEMS support the leaves and flowers. The tubes inside the stem carry water upwards from the ground.

3 The LEAVES are most important. They contain chlorophyll, a green-colored chemical, which reacts with sunlight to make food for the plant.

How do plants reproduce?

1 Attracted by its smell, or wanting to taste its delicious nectar, insects buzz around inside a flower. Powdery grains, called POLLEN, rub off the male parts of the flower (called STAMENS) and onto the insects.

2 The insects fly to another flower where the pollen is left on the female parts, called PISTILS.

3 This is how SEEDS are produced. New plants will develop and grow to be just like their parents.

Notice the beautiful markings on this monarch butterfly.

A bee sitting on a thistle.

Sensational Seeds!

Seeds are amazing things—they have developed all sorts of ways to find new places to grow. Here's how they do it...

Fruit and vegetable seeds

Many seeds are contained inside the soft flesh of fruit and veg. This protects them and keeps them fed and moist until they start to grow. Apples, oranges, avocados, peas, and lots of others contain seeds (often called "pips") which drop to the ground when the fruit ripens.

Flying seeds

Some seeds rely on the wind to carry them to new soil. Dandelion seeds are a good example. The wind removes the cluster of

Dandelion seeds flying in the wind.

light, fluffy seeds from the dandelion head and sends them floating away on the breeze. Sycamore trees do something similar, though their seeds have two wings that let them spin through the air like tiny helicopters.

A variety of fruit and vegetables—apples, pears, avocados, zucchini, and green beans.

Sycamore seeds.

Animal-friendly seeds

Seeds are also moved around by animals. Berries are the favourite food of many birds who peck at the fruit and carry the seeds away in their beaks.

Acorns— the seeds of an oak tree.

A grey squirrel feeding on an acorn.

Squirrels love collecting acorns for their winter food stores. They hide them away, but sometimes forget where! These forgotten acorns will grow into oak trees.

Sticky seeds

Some seeds are prickly or sticky so that they cling to the skin or fur of passing animals. Burdock seeds, for example, have tiny hooks that enable them to latch on to anything that touches them!

Succeeding with seeds

Remember these points when you grow your seeds and you're sure to be successful.

1 Seeds need good soil in which to grow.

2 When a seed sprouts, it is called germination. To help your seeds to germinate, put your propagator in a warm, dark place.

3 Water is also needed to make your seeds sprout. Just keep the soil moist. Soaking them is as bad as not watering them at all!

4 When your seeds start to grow, move the propagator to a windowsill to give them lots of light.

5 When your seeds have grown into seedlings, transfer them into flowerpots so they can grow into big plants.

Get Your Hair Cut!

Growing mustard and cress trolls

Mustard and cress seeds grow very quickly. You can use them to make funny-faced people with hair that really grows!

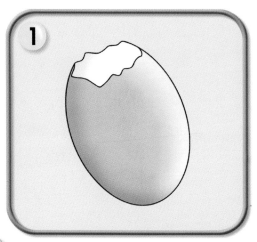

You will need:
- eggshells
- egg cups
- mustard and cress seeds
- absorbent cotton
- felt-tip pens or acrylic paints
- a water-sprayer

1 Have a boiled egg for breakfast. Be careful how you break open the top. Keep the empty shell.

2 Draw, or paint, a face on your eggshell. Make your troll look as funny or scary as you can.

3 Dampen some absorbent cotton with water and press it gently into the shell.

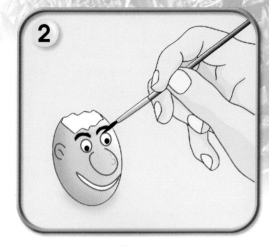

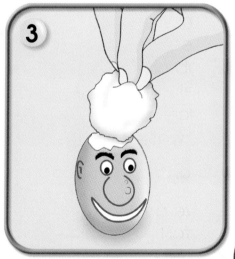

4 Sprinkle some mustard and cress seeds onto the cotton and place it in a warm, dark place.

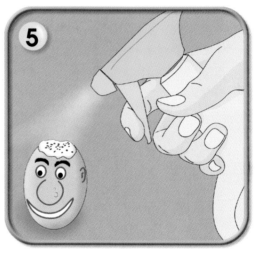

5 Spray some more water on from time to time so the absorbent cotton doesn't dry out.

6 When your seeds start to sprout, bring them out into the light. You will find your troll now has green hair growing out of the top of his head!

One more thing...

When your troll's hair gets really long, you can give him a trim!

What's in a Name?

Growing mustard and cress letters

You can grow your initials, your name (if it is short) or your age with mustard and cress seeds.

1 Spread a sheet of blotting paper over the bottom of the tray. Make sure it goes right to the edges.

You will need:
- propagator from your kit
- watering can
- mustard and cress seeds
- blotting paper

2 Water the blotting paper until it is really soaked.

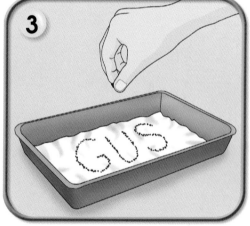

3 Sprinkle the seeds onto the blotting paper, carefully making shapes of the letters or numbers that you want.

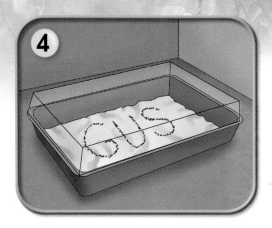

4 Put the lid of the propagator onto the tray. Place in a warm, dark place so the seeds can start growing.

5 Take out and water every day—the blotting paper must stay wet all the time.

6 After sprouting, put the propagator in a light place like a windowsill. Watch your special letters or numbers grow bigger every day!

One more thing...

When the mustard and cress is fully grown, you can cut it and use it to make tasty sandwiches. Remember— mustard tastes hot! If you don't like that, use more of the cress than the mustard.

23

What a Topping Idea!

Growing vegetable hats

Not everything grows from small seeds. Plants also grow out of vegetables. You can see this by growing some plant-top hats.

Warning…
NEEDS ADULT HELP!
Ask an adult to cut the vegetables for you.

You will need:
- a watering can or pitcher
- shallow containers like old saucers or plates
- any of the following vegetables—carrot, parsnip, turnip, radish, or fresh beet
- a chopping block
- a knife (for an adult to use)
- small gravel for decoration

1 When you go to the grocery store or supermarket, buy one or two extra carrots and parsnips.

2 Ask an adult to cut the tops off for you. The tops only need to be about an inch tall.

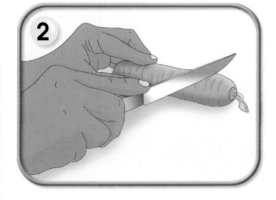

3 Arrange the tops on the saucers or plates. You can keep the different vegetables separate or mix them up to see which top grows the quickest.

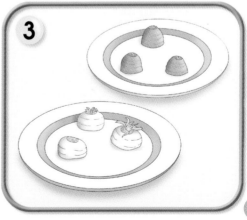

4 Sprinkle gravel round the tops. (You don't have to do this, but it makes the plants look much neater and helps to keep the water round them.)

5 Water your plant tops, but don't flood them. Keep them watered every day.

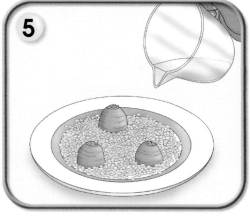

6 Put them in a warm place. They should grow pretty hats within two to three weeks.

One more thing...

You don't need to do any cutting or planting if you use a potato or an onion. Just leave them somewhere dry and warm for a few weeks and they will sprout shoots and roots all by themselves!

Beans Means Fun!

Growing beans in a mini observatory

Most plants grow underground where you can't see what's happening. This way of growing beans lets you see everything— roots, shoots, the lot!

1 Place the yogurt pot upside down inside the jar.

You will need:
- a watering can
- a clean, empty jar
- an empty yogurt pot
- a sheet of blotting paper
- runner bean seeds

2 Roll the blotting paper into a tube and push it into the jar. The yogurt pot should keep it in place and pressed against the sides.

3 Carefully push five or six bean seeds down between the blotting paper and the glass. They need to stop about half-way, not right at the bottom.

4 Pour water into the jar until it is about one quarter full.

5 Put the seeds in a warm place, like above a radiator or on a sunny windowsill.

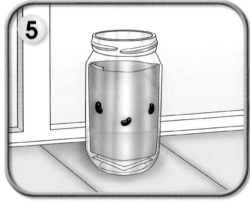

6 Check your mini observatory every day to see the shoots growing up and the roots growing down.

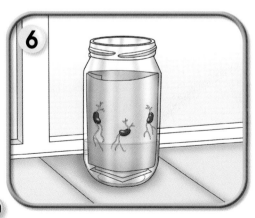

One more thing...

If you want to feel like a real scientist, make a growth chart for your beans. You can record information such as which bean has sprouted first, which bean has grown the biggest, how long the roots and shoots are, and so on.

Salad Days

Growing tasty herbs

Here's how to grow some delicious herbs to flavor a summer salad...
or give your pussycat a really yummy treat!

You will need:
- propagator from your kit
- dibble from your kit
- tags and stickers from your kit
- a watering can
- compost
- basil, chives, and dill seeds (for the salad)
- catnip seeds (for the cat treat)

1 Fill your propagator to within half an inch of the top with compost.

2 Moisten the compost and use your dibble to make some rows of shallow holes.

3 Drop a few of the same kind of seeds into each row. Mark the different rows clearly, using the tags.

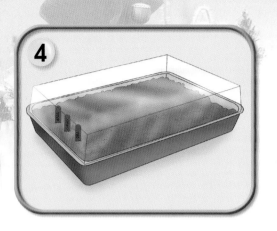

4 Put the lid on the propagator and keep it warm until the seeds have germinated.

5 Then move it to a light windowsill and keep it moist. When the seedlings are big and strong, put them in flowerpots or plant outside.

6 When the basil, chives, and dill are fully grown, remove some of the leaves and wash thoroughly. Ask an adult to chop the leaves up and sprinkle them over lettuce, tomato and cucumber for a new salad sensation. If you grow the catnip, put a little into your cat's food. He or she will smell it a mile away and come running. Cats go crazy for catnip!

Sunflower Power

Sunflower races and competitions

Sunflowers grow huge in a very short time. Use them to have fun with your friends. Whose grows the fastest? Whose grows the tallest?

You will need:
- sunflower seeds
- tall garden canes
- string
- a trowel
- a large outdoor watering can

1 Ask an adult for permission to use a flower bed in the garden. Sunflowers grow best in front of a wall or fence.

2 If the flower bed is overgrown, ask an adult to help you dig it. The soil needs to be soft and loose, and free of stones.

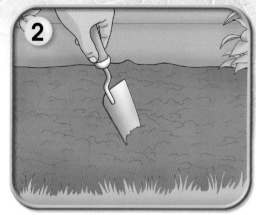

3 Plant the seeds one by one, leaving a space of about 12 in. between them.

⚠️ **Warning...**
NEEDS ADULT HELP!
Ask an adult to help you dig and push canes into the ground.

If you don't have a garden, try growing the seeds in pots on a windowsill.

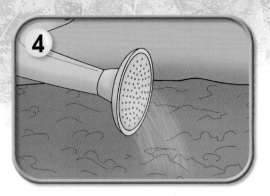

4 Water the flower bed every day. The first shoots should appear in about two weeks.

5 If you have too many baby plants, pull out the weak ones. This gives room for the strong ones to grow.

6 As the sunflowers get really big, push the canes into the ground and tie string round the stems. This stops the tall flowers falling over.

One more thing...

When you've decided who's won the competitions, don't throw your dead sunflowers away. Take the seeds from the middle of the flowers and feed them to the birds. Also, keep a few for yourself so you can have another contest next year!

One... Two... Tree!

Growing a tree from seed

This is a very exciting thing to do provided you're happy to wait a long time. Trees take ages to grow. If you start one early and look after it for years, you could have a tree for life!

You will need:
- flowerpots from your kit
- dibble from your kit
- tags and labels from your kit
- a watering can
- compost
- a mixing bowl
- fruit seeds such as apple, orange, or avocado
- tree seeds such as acorns, chestnuts, or sycamore seeds
- plastic freezer bags

1 Pour some compost into the mixing bowl and gradually add some water. Keep stirring until the compost is moist right through.

2 Spoon the compost into your flowerpots and make a hole in the middle with your dibble. It needs to be about half an inch deep.

3 Plant the seed of your choice. Mark it using the tags and stickers.

4 Cover each pot with a plastic bag and store them in a warm, dark place until some shoots appear.

5 When the shoots are big and strong, take off the plastic bag and put your baby tree on a sunny windowsill. Keep watering... but not too much!

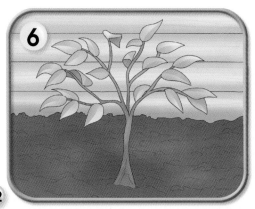

6 When your tree has grown too big for the flowerpot, transfer it to a bigger one or plant it somewhere suitable outdoors.

One more thing...

One day, your seed could grow into a mighty tree, so plant it in an open space to allow it plenty of room to grow.

Make sure it is not too near your house otherwise its leaves may block out the light and its roots could do damage beneath your home.

43

Plants for Prezzies!

Growing hyacinths in a decorated pot

Hyacinths have a wonderful smell! Grow them in a flowerpot you've decorated and you have the perfect present for someone in your family!

You will need:
- a watering can or jug
- a saucer
- a terra cotta flowerpot (don't use a plastic one from your kit)
- acrylic paints
- compost
- one, two or three hyacinth bulbs (depending on the size of the pot)
- colored ribbon

1 Wash and dry your flowerpot to make sure it's perfectly clean.

2 Paint colorful patterns on the flowerpot. Leave the paint to dry completely.

3 Fill the flowerpot with potting compost almost to the top.

4 Put the hyacinth bulbs into the compost. Don't bury them too deeply—they grow best with about a quarter still showing at the top.

5 Place in a saucer and water well. Keep watered until you are ready to give as a gift.

6 Tie the ribbon around the pot as a pretty finishing touch.

One more thing...

You can also buy see-through containers that hold a single hyacinth bulb at the top. When filled with water, you see all the long white roots growing down from the bulb. These also make good presents for a gardening-mad friend.

There's More!

Why not try these other great ideas?

Tom Thumb's garden

Make your own miniature garden on a tray.
Use a mirror for a pond and decorate it with
little plants that you have grown or bought.

Butterfly garden

Ask an adult for permission to use one
small corner of the garden. Encourage
the plants in it to grow wild by watering
them and leaving them alone. You'll
find that butterflies are attracted to
the flowers in your overgrown garden.

Grow your own vegetable soup

Use your kit to grow some vegetables
from seed, then ask an adult
to help you make some
delicious vegetable soup.